What's Up, Beanie?

aCUTEly relatable comics

by Alina Tysoe

Houghton Mifflin Harcourt   Boston New York 2021

4

Baby Beanie

Snails

A Beret

11

Stealthy

Candy

Sleepy Creepy

My Family

Mama knows where all the good food is—

—and also gives the BEST hugs.

Squiiish!

hehe

haha haha

We do NOT bother her when she's gardening. It's the RULES.

That's Papa.

Papa is SO tall that he can reach the top bookshelf AND touch the ceiling whenever he wants to!

hehe

He can also fall asleep ANYWHERE and in exactly 3 seconds.

...

SNOOOOORE

See?

This is my oldest sister! She can make animals out of paper!

Magic!!

She also has the longest hair and lets me play hairdresser!

19

Snuggle

Dalmatian

Kindergarten

Ouch

23

Duvet

Birthday Bunny

Lunch Cereal

Career Dreams

Baby Logic

Chaotic Sleeper

Moustache

First Snow

Tiny Spoon

Tomato Love

New Kitten

Pet Respect

41

Waiting

Bathtime

43

Cow Friends

Sleeping Method

Baby Beanie's Method For Sleeping Alone in the Dark.

Step 1: Cocoon Self in Blanket

Step 2: Face the Wall

(Because seeing the room is too scary and denial is the only way to fall asleep.)

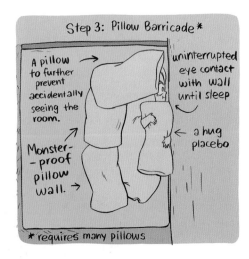

Step 3: Pillow Barricade *

A pillow to further prevent accidentally seeing the room.

Monster-proof pillow wall. →

uninterrupted eye contact with wall until sleep

← a hug placebo

* requires many pillows

47

Lizard

49

Mountains

Bunk Bed

Car Naps

Suspicious Silence

Hide and Seek

oldest sister

HIDE AND SEEK!!!!

Okay, okay jeez.

SIGH... One... Two... Three...

skitter skitter skitter

Four, five, six, seven, eight, nine...

Ten...

Oh nooo where did you go?

giggle giggle

You're too good at hiding! It's not fair!!!

hehe

55

The Power

Bedtime Stories

Make Believe

Sailor Beanie

Your hair isn't yellow...

T-that's because...

It's a disguise!

...

OOOOOOoo

Hey Sailor Moon! Is Tuxedo Mask your boyfriend?

It's a secret.

yes.

You're so cool!

Concert

Food Method

Mushroom Soup

scrape scrape scrape

Oh! Are you guys done?

Yeah! Mmm it was so good.

Ye

Why are there so many mushrooms in the pot ???!

We should've flushed them down the toilet!

65

Not Mama

Learning to Read

Piano

Morning Sneak

Portrait

Birthdays

Hey, Mama?

Yeah?

older sister's birthday cake

Birthday people get cake and all the presents, right?

Yep!

hmmm.

Later

Be right back.

Okay!

nop

Power Outage

Bread Mouse

Strawberries

Dress Up

Caterpillar

-the caterpillar thought too hard about how to walk with her many legs and got them all confused and tangled!

Hm...

That's silly!

Oh yeah? Sometimes it can be hard to do something when you overthink it!

Even walking?

Yeah!

Silly!

Haha. Well what do YOU do with your arms when you walk?

EASY!

You just-

Move them...

...

Um...? Right? Left leg...?

? 2+2 ? Left... No...

Mama's Food

Backstory

Day Nap

Suddenly missing Mama and scared of Papa's snoring.

Snow Day

Olives

Scary Hallways

Mission "Window"

Left Behind

Socks

Bonk!

Baby Cabbage

Toy Surprise

Childhood Games

Change

Everything

Teen Beanie

Cooking with Mama

Nighttime Snacks

Speaking English

Washing Dishes

Embarassment

Snack Sense

Cleaning

Drowsy

Beanie, why don't you answer the next questi—

COUGH!!!

Favorite Song

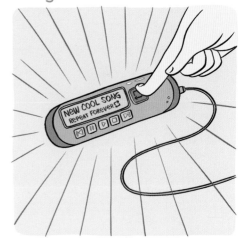

Alarm

Speech

Loner Lunch

Friendship Progress

Goodbye School

Adult Beanie

Whack!

131

3 AM Crafts

133

Talking to People

Why do you actively avoid talking to people?

Because when I talk I reveal too much about myself then people figure out that I'm weird and push me away. I fear and avoid rejection.

LoL idk just shy I guess?

You can never know the real me.

Trash

Dear Diary

137

Puppy Guilt

Cold Nose Boop

Cute Things That Dogs Do

① The lean and sigh

sigh

② The Zoomies

hehe

③ Curling into a little cuddle donut ♡

④ This.

sploot

Puppy Energy

Puppy Sparkles

More Cute Things About Dogs

Cat Cuddles

Happy Socks

Mike

Puppy Betrayal

Saying Hello

SAYING HELLO TO AN ACQUAINTANCE

VS SAYING HELLO TO A BESTIE

Tasty

Party Puppy

Phone Calls

Party Rude

Watch Together

157

Confessions

Cookies and Tea Beach Date

This is so nice.

I better not ruin it by being too forward.

Can't rush too much with my feelings-

Hmm

Hey-

Bonnie

Come meet my parents' new puppy!

!

Isn't she so cute? We called her Bonnie.

Such a good girl!

Oh hey Beanie! How are you?

Mike was just telling us about—

Err... Hello?

Hello? Beanie, are you ok

Beanie?

Is she okay...?

Yeah just give her a moment

Seal

Puppy Distraction

Toot

Dinner Decisions

Not Sleeping

Snoring

Telephone Persona

Must Clean

Woah! The apartment is so clean!

Ta daaaa!!

I organised the shelves!

Ooooo

All the socks have pairs!

Amazing.

Wait.

Did you finish that important e-mail you had to write?

hey-

SCRUB

SCRUB

SCRUB

SCRUB

MUST CLEAAAAN

Music Shame

Books

Work Music

Decision

Proposal

Sleep-in Accomplice

Blanket Thief

Sleep Fears

Onion Memory

Kiss the Girl

Wedding Dress

Skewed

Wedding

186

Spice

Nostalgic Tunes

Support

Unreachable Puppies

Layers of Mess

Airport Goodbyes

New Start

Beanie's new job

I'M READY!

. . .

STRIDE STRIDE

I-I feel sick.

NOPE

Aw! It's going to be okay!

Cold Glasses

Blizzard Day

Cocoon

Calling Home

Exercise

Friendship Feelings

Volume

Tickle

Over-Politeness Loop

Game Decisions

Bed Thief

Planner Fail

Sleep Talking

Selfies

Midnight Potatoes

Cheese Time

Wishing for Puppies

214

Dreaming of Puppies

Stolen Kiss

Sit Together

Well OF COURSE you've learnt stuff. I'm amazing.

haha

Most importantly though—

Before I head back to my time, do you have any old-person wisdom for me?

hmmm...

old person...?

People will try and make decisions for you, and they won't have your best interest in mind.

You need to think for yourself and figure out what's best for you.

hmm ok.

- To my family ♡

Library of Congress Cataloging-in-Publication Data
Names: Tysoe, Alina, author, illustrator.
Title: What's up, Beanie? : acutely relatable comics / by Alina Tysoe.
Description: Boston : Houghton Mifflin Harcourt, 2021.
Identifiers: LCCN 2020057697 (print) | LCCN 2020057698 (ebook) | ISBN
9780358455486 (hardback) | ISBN 9780358447788 (ebook)
Subjects: LCSH: Graphic novels. | CYAC: Graphic novels. | Humorous stories.
Classification: LCC PZ7.7.T97 Wh 2021 (print) | LCC PZ7.7.T97 (ebook) |
DDC 741.5/973—dc23
LC record available at https://lccn.loc.gov/2020057697
LC ebook record available at https://lccn.loc.gov/2020057698

Printed in China

SCP 10 9 8 7 6 5 4 3 2 1